The Great War in England in 1897

BY

WILLIAM LE QUEX

British Library Cataloguing-in-Publication Data
A catalogue record for this book is available from the
British Library

CONTENTS

WILLIAM LE QUEUX

William Tufnell Le Queux was born in London in 1864. He was educated at various institutions in Europe, before writing for a number of French newspapers. In the late 1880s, he returned to England and edited the magazines *Gossip* and *Piccadilly*, before joining *The Globe* in 1891 as a parliamentary reporter. Two years later, he quit journalism, to concentrate fully on writing fiction. Over the rest of his life, Le Queux was a hugely prolific writer, best-known for his two works of 'invasion literature' *The Great War in England in 1897* (1894) and *The Invasion of 1910* (1906) (which a huge success, selling more than a million copies). Eventually, Le Queux penned a total of 150 novels, before dying in Knokke, Belgium in 1927, aged 63.

THE GREAT WAR IN ENGLAND IN 1897

William Le Quex

LOOTING IN THE SUBURBS!

While famished men crept into Hyde Park and Kensington Gardens and there expired under the trees of absolute hunger, and starving women with babes at their breasts sank upon doorsteps and died, the more robust Londoners had, on hearing of the enemy's march on the metropolis, gone south to augment the second line of defence. For several weeks huge barricades had been thrown up in the principal roads approaching London from the south. The strongest of these were opposite the Convalescent Home on Kingston Hill, in Coombe Lane close to Raynes Park Station, in the Morden Road at Merton Abbey, opposite Lynwood in the Tooting Road; while nearer London, on the same road, there was a strong one with machine guns on the crest of Balham Hill, and another in Clapham Road. At Streatham Hill, about one hundred yards from the hospital, earthworks had been thrown up, and several guns brought into position; while at

Beulah Hill, Norwood, opposite the Post Office at Upper Sydenham, at the Half Moon at Herne Hill, and in many of the roads between Honor Oak and Denmark Hill, barricades had been constructed and banked up with bags and baskets filled with earth.

Though these defences were held by enthusiastic civilians of all classes—professional men, artisans, and tradesmen—yet our second line of defence, distinct, of course, from the local barricades, was a very weak one. We had relied upon our magnificent strategic positions on the Surrey Hills, and had not made sufficient provision in case of a sudden reverse. Our second line, stretching from Croydon up to South Norwood, thence to Streatham and along the railway line to Wimbledon and Kingston, was composed of a few battalions of Volunteers, detachments of Metropolitan police, Berks and Bucks constabulary, London firemen and postmen, the Corps of Commissionaires—in fact, every body of drilled men who could be requisitioned to handle revolver or rifle. These were backed by great bodies of civilians, and behind stood the barricades with their insignificant-looking but terribly deadly machine guns.

The railways had, on the first news of the enemy's success at Leatherhead and Guildford, all been cut up, and in each of the many bridges spanning the Thames between Kingston and the Tower great charges of gun-cotton had been placed, so that they might be blown up at any instant, and thus prevent the enemy from investing the city.

Day dawned again at last—dull and grey. It had rained during the night, and the roads, wet and muddy, were unutterably gloomy as our civilian defenders looked out upon them, well knowing that ere long a fierce attack would be made. In the night the enemy had been busy laying a field telegraph from Mitcham to Kingston, through which messages were now being continually flashed.

Suddenly, just as the British outposts were being relieved, the French commenced a vigorous attack, and in a quarter of an hour fighting extended along the whole line. Volunteers, firemen, policemen, Commissionaires, and civilians all fought bravely, trusting to one hope, namely, that before they were defeated the enemy would be outflanked and attacked in their rear by a British force from the Surrey Hills. They well knew that to effectually bar the advance of this great body of French was out of all question, yet they fought on with creditable tact, and in many instances inflicted serious loss upon the enemy's infantry.

Soon, however, French field guns were trained upon them, and amid the roar of artillery line after line of heroic Britons fell shattered to earth. Amid the rattle of musketry, the crackling of the machine guns, and the booming of sixteen-pounders, brave Londoners struggled valiantly against the masses of wildly excited Frenchmen; yet every moment the line became slowly weakened, and the defenders were gradually forced back upon their barricades. The resistance which the French met with was much more determined than they had anticipated; in fact, a small force of Volunteers holding the Mitcham Road, at Streatham, fought with such splendid bravery, that they succeeded alone and unaided in completely wiping out a battalion of French infantry, and capturing two field guns and a quantity of ammunition. For this success, however, they, alas! paid dearly, for a quarter of an hour later a large body of cavalry and infantry coming over from Woodlands descended upon them and totally annihilated them, with the result that Streatham fell into the hands of the French, and a few guns placed in the high road soon made short work of the earthworks near the hospital. Under the thick hail of bursting shells the brave band who manned the guns were at last compelled to abandon them, and the enemy were soon marching unchecked into Stockwell and Brixton, extending their right, with the majority of their artillery, across Herne Hill, Dulwich, and Honor Oak.

In the meantime a desperate battle was being fought around Kingston. The barricade on Kingston Hill held out for nearly three hours, but was at last captured by the invaders, and of those who had manned it not a man survived. Mitcham and Tooting had fallen in the first hour of the engagement, the barricade at Lynwood had been taken, and hundreds of the houses in Balham had been looted by the enemy in their advance into Clapham.

Nearly the whole morning it rained in torrents, and both invaders and defenders were wet to the skin, and covered with blood and mud. Everywhere British pluck showed itself in this desperate resistance on the part of these partially-trained defenders. At the smaller barricades in the suburban jerry-built streets, Britons held their own and checked the advance with remarkable coolness; yet, as the dark, stormy day wore on, the street defences were one after another broken down and destroyed.

Indeed, by three o'clock that afternoon the enemy ran riot through the whole district, from Lower Sydenham to Kingston. Around the larger houses on Sydenham Hill one of the fiercest fights occurred, but at length the defenders were driven down into Lordship Lane, and the houses on the hill were sacked, and some of them burned. While this was proceeding, a great force of French artillery came over from Streatham, and before dusk five great batteries had been established along the Parade in front of the Crystal Palace, and on Sydenham Hill and One Tree Hill; while other smaller batteries were brought into position at Forest Hill, Gipsy Hill, Tulse Hill, Streatham Hill and Herne Hill; and further towards London about twenty French twelve-pounders and a number of new quick-firing weapons of long range and a very destructive character were placed along the top of Camberwell Grove and Denmark Hill.

The defences of London had been broken. The track of the invaders was marked by ruined homes and heaps of corpses, and London's millions knew on this eventful night that the enemy were now actually at their doors. In Fleet Street, in the Strand, in Piccadilly, the news spread from mouth to mouth as darkness fell that the enemy were preparing to launch their deadly shells into the City. This increased the panic. The people were in a mad frenzy of excitement, and the scenes everywhere were terrible. Women wept and wailed, men uttered words of blank despair, and children screamed at an unknown terror.

The situation was terrible. From the Embankment away on the Surrey side could be seen a lurid glare in the sky. It was the reflection of a great fire in Vassall Road, Brixton, the whole street being burned by the enemy, together with the great block of houses lying between the Cowley and Brixton Roads.

London waited. Dark storm-clouds scudded across the moon. The chill wind swept up the river, and moaned mournfully in doors and chimneys.

At last, without warning, just as Big Ben had boomed forth one o'clock, the thunder of artillery shook the windows, and startled the excited crowds. Great shells crashed into the streets, remained for a second, and then burst with deafening report and appalling effect.

In Trafalgar Square, Fleet Street, and the Strand the deadly projectiles commenced to fall thickly, wrecking the shops, playing havoc with the public buildings, and sweeping hundreds of men and women into eternity. Nothing could withstand their awful force, and the people, rushing madly about like frightened sheep, felt that this was indeed their last hour.

In Ludgate Hill the scene was awful, Shots fell with monotonous regularity, bursting everywhere, and blowing buildings and men into atoms. The French shells were terribly devastating; the reek of mélinite poisoned the air. Shells striking St Paul's Cathedral brought down the right-hand tower, and crashed into the dome; while others set on fire a long range of huge drapery warehouses behind it, the glare of the roaring flames causing the great black Cathedral to stand out in bold relief.

The bombardment had actually commenced! London, the proud Capital of the World, was threatened with destruction!

LONDON BOMBARDED

The Hand of the Destroyer had reached England's mighty metropolis. The lurid scene was appalling.

In the stormy sky the red glare from hundreds of burning buildings grew brighter, and in every quarter flames leaped up and black smoke curled slowly away in increasing volume.

The people were unaware of the events that had occurred in Surrey that day. Exhausted, emaciated, and ashen pale, the hungry people had endured every torture. Panic-stricken, they rushed hither and thither in thousands up and down the principal thoroughfares, and as they tore headlong away in this *sauve qui peut* to the northern suburbs, the weaker fell and were trodden under foot.

Men fought for their wives and families, dragging them away out of the range of the enemy's fire, which apparently did not extend beyond the line formed by the Hackney Road, City Road, Pentonville Road, Euston Road, and Westbourne Park. But in that terrible rush to escape many delicate ladies were crushed to death, and numbers of others, with their children, sank exhausted, and perished beneath the feet of the fleeing millions.

Never before had such alarm been spread through London; never before had such awful scenes of destruction been witnessed. The French Commander-in-Chief, who was senior to his Russian colleague, had been killed, and his successor being unwilling to act in concert with the Muscovite staff, a quarrel ensued. It was this quarrel which caused the bombardment of London, totally against the instructions of their respective Governments. The bombardment was, in fact, wholly unnecessary, and was in a great measure due to some confused orders received by the French General from his Commander-in-Chief. Into the midst of the surging, terrified crowds that congested the streets on each side of the Thames, shells filled with mélinite dropped, and, bursting, blew hundreds of despairing Londoners to atoms. Houses were shattered and fell, public buildings were demolished, factories were set alight, and the powerful exploding projectiles caused the Great City to reel and quake. Above the constant crash of bursting shells, the dull roar of the flames, and the crackling of burning timbers, terrific detonations now and then were heard, as buildings, filled with combustibles, were struck by shots, and, exploding, spread death and ruin over wide areas. The centre of commerce, of wealth, of intellectual and moral life was being ruthlessly wrecked, and its inhabitants massacred. Apparently it was not the intention of the enemy to invest the city at present, fearing perhaps that the force that had penetrated the defences was not sufficiently large to accomplish such a gigantic task;

therefore they had commenced this terrible bombardment as a preliminary measure.

Through the streets of South London the people rushed along, all footsteps being bent towards the bridges; but on every one of them the crush was frightful—indeed, so great was it that in several instances the stone balustrades were broken, and many helpless, shrieking persons were forced over into the dark swirling waters below. The booming of the batteries was continuous, the bursting of the shells was deafening, and every moment was one of increasing horror. Men saw their homes swept away, and trembling women clung to their husbands, speechless with fear. In the City, in the Strand, in Westminster, and West End streets the ruin was even greater, and the destruction of property enormous.

Westward, both great stations at Victoria, with the adjoining furniture repositories and the Grosvenor Hotel, were burning fiercely; while the Wellington Barracks had been partially demolished, and the roof of St Peter's Church blown away. Two shells falling in the quadrangle of Buckingham Palace had smashed every window and wrecked some of the ground-floor apartments, but nevertheless upon the flagstaff, amidst the dense smoke and showers of sparks flying upward, there still floated the Royal Standard. St James's Palace, Marlborough House, Stafford House, and Clarence House, standing in exposed positions, were being all more or less damaged; several houses in Carlton House Terrace had been partially demolished, and a shell striking the Duke of York's Column soon after the commencement of the bombardment, caused it to fall, blocking Waterloo Place.

Time after time shells whistled above and fell with a crash and explosion, some in the centre of the road, tearing up the paving, and others striking the clubs in Pall Mall, blowing out many of those noble time-mellowed walls. The portico of the Athenaeum had been torn away like pasteboard, the rear premises of the War Office had been pulverized, and the Carlton, Reform, and United Service Clubs suffered terrible damage. Two shells striking the Junior Carlton crashed through the roof, and exploding almost simultaneously, brought down an enormous heap of masonry, which fell across the roadway, making an effectual barricade; while at the same moment shells began to fall thickly in Grosvenor Place and Belgrave Square, igniting many houses, and killing some of those who remained in their homes petrified by fear.

Up Regent Street shells were sweeping with frightful effect. The Café Monico and the whole block of buildings surrounding it was burning, and the flames leaping high, presented a magnificent though appalling spectacle. The front of the London Pavilion had been partially blown away, and of the two uniform rows of shops forming the Quadrant many had been wrecked. From Air Street to Oxford Circus, and along Piccadilly to Knightsbridge, there fell a perfect hail of shells and bullets. Devonshire House had been wrecked; and the Burlington Arcade destroyed. The thin pointed spire of St James's Church had fallen, every window in the Albany was shattered, several houses in Grosvenor Place had suffered considerably, and a shell that struck the southern side of St George's Hospital had ignited it, and now at 2 a.m., in the midst of this awful scene of destruction and disaster, the helpless sick were being removed into the open streets, where bullets whistled about them and fragments of explosive shells whizzed past.

As the night wore on London trembled and fell. Once Mistress of the World, she was now, alas! sinking under the iron hand of the invader. Upon her there poured a rain of deadly missiles that caused appalling slaughter and desolation. The newly introduced long-range guns, and the terrific power of the explosives with which the French shells were charged, added to the horrors of the bombardment; for although the batteries were so far away as to be out of sight, yet the unfortunate people, overtaken by their doom, were torn limb from limb by the bursting bombs.

Over the roads lay men of London, poor and rich, weltering in their blood, their lower limbs shattered or blown completely away. With wide-open haggard eyes, in their death agony they gazed around at the burning buildings, at the falling débris, and upward at the brilliantly-illumined sky. With their last breath they gasped prayers for those they loved, and sank to the grave, hapless victims of Babylon's downfall.

Every moment the Great City was being devastated, every moment the catastrophe was more complete, more awful. In the poorer quarters of South London whole streets were swept away, and families overwhelmed by their own demolished homes. Along the principal thoroughfares shop fronts were shivered, and the goods displayed in the windows strewn about the roadway.

About half past three a frightful disaster occurred at Battersea. Very few shells had dropped in that district, when suddenly one fell right in the very centre of a great petroleum store. The effect was frightful. With a noise that was heard for twenty miles around, the whole of the great store of oil exploded, blowing the stores themselves high into the air, and levelling all the buildings in the vicinity. In every direction burning oil was projected over the roofs of neighbouring houses, dozens of which at once caught fire, while down the streets there ran great streams of blazing oil, which spread the conflagration in every direction. Showers of sparks flew upwards, the flames roared and crackled, and soon fires were breaking out in all quarters.

Just as the clocks were striking a quarter to four, a great shell struck the Victoria Tower of the Houses of Parliament, bringing it down with a terrific crash. This disaster was quickly followed by a series of others. A shell fell through the roof of Westminster Abbey, setting the grand old historic building on fire; another tore away the columns from the front of the Royal Exchange; and a third carried away one of the square twin towers of St Mary Woolnoth, at the corner of Lombard Street.

Along this latter thoroughfare banks were wrecked, and offices set on fire; while opposite, in the thick walls of the Bank of England, great breaches were being made. The Mansion House escaped any very serious injury, but the dome of the Stock Exchange was carried away; and in Queen Victoria Street, from end to end, enormous damage was caused to the rows of fine business premises; while further east the Monument, broken in half, came down with a noise like thunder, demolishing many houses on Fish Street Hill.

The great drapery warehouses in Wood Street, Bread Street, Friday Street, Foster Lane, and St Paul's Churchyard suffered more or less. Ryland's, Morley's, and Cook's were all alight and burning fiercely; while others were wrecked and shattered, and their contents blown out into the streets. The quaint spire of St Bride's had fallen, and its bells lay among the débris in the adjoining courts; both the half-wrecked offices of the *Daily Telegraph* and the *Daily Chronicle* were being consumed.

The great clock-tower of the Law Courts fell about four o'clock with a terrific crash, completely blocking the Strand at Temple Bar, and demolishing the much-abused Griffin Memorial; while at the same moment two large holes were torn in the roof of the Great Hall, the small black turret above fell, and the whole of the glass in the building was shivered into fragments.

It was amazing how widespread was the ruin caused by each of the explosive missiles. Considering the number of guns employed by the French in this cruel and wanton destruction of property, the desolation they were causing was enormous. This was owing to the rapid extension of their batteries over the high ground from One Tree Hill through Peckham to Greenwich, and more especially to the wide ranges of their guns and the terrific power of their shells. In addition to the ordinary projectiles filled with mélinite, charges of that extremely powerful substance lignine dynamite were hurled into the city, and, exploded by a detonator, swept away whole streets, and laid many great public buildings in ruins; while steel shells, filled with some arrangement of liquid oxygen and blasting gelatine, produced frightful effects, for nothing could withstand them.

One of these, discharged from the battery on Denmark Hill, fell in the quadrangle behind Burlington House, and levelled the Royal Academy and the surrounding buildings. Again a terrific explosion sounded, and as the smoke cleared it was seen that a gelatine shell had fallen among the many turrets of the Natural History Museum, and the front of the building fell out with a deafening crash, completely blocking the Cromwell Road.

London lay at the mercy of the invaders. So swiftly had the enemy cut their way through the defences and opened their hail of destroying missiles, that the excited, starving populace were unaware of what had occurred until dynamite began to rain upon them. Newspapers had ceased to appear; and although telegraphic communication was kept up with the defenders on the Surrey Hills by the War Office, yet no details of the events occurring there had been made public for fear of spies. Londoners had remained in ignorance, and, alas! had awaited their doom. Through the long sultry night the situation was one of indescribable panic and disaster.

The sky had grown a brighter red, and the streets within the range of the enemy's guns, now deserted, were in most cases blocked by burning ruins and fallen telegraph wires; while about the roadways lay the shattered corpses of men, women, and children, upon whom the shells had wrought their frightful work.

The bodies, mutilated, torn limb from limb, were sickening to gaze upon.

BABYLON BURNING

Dynamite had shattered Charing Cross Station and the Hotel, for its smoke-begrimed façade had been torn out, and the station yard was filled with a huge pile of smouldering débris. On either side of the Strand from Villiers Street to Temple Bar scarcely a window had been left intact, and the roadway itself was quite impassable, for dozens of buildings had been overthrown by shells, and what in many cases had been handsome shops were now heaps of bricks, slates, furniture, and twisted girders. The rain of fire continued. Dense black smoke rising in a huge column from St Martin's Church showed plainly what was the fate of that noble edifice, while fire had now broken out at the Tivoli Music Hall, and the clubs on Adelphi Terrace were also falling a prey to the flames.

The burning of Babylon was a sight of awful, appalling grandeur.

The few people remaining in the vicinity of the Strand who escaped the flying missiles and falling buildings, sought what shelter they could, and stood petrified by terror, knowing that every moment might be their last, not daring to fly into the streets leading to Holborn, where they could see the enemy's shells were still falling with unabated regularity and frightful result, their courses marked by crashing buildings and blazing ruins.

Looking from Charing Cross, the Strand seemed one huge glaring furnace. Flames belched from windows on either side, and, bursting through roofs, great tongues of fire shot upwards; blazing timbers fell into the street; and as the buildings became gutted, and the fury of the devouring element was spent, shattered walls tottered and fell into the roadway. The terrific heat, the roar of the flames, the blinding smoke, the stifling fumes of dynamite, the pungent, poisonous odour of mélinite, the clouds of dust, the splinters of stone and steel, and the constant bursting of shells, combined to render the scene the most awful ever witnessed in a single thoroughfare during the history of the world.

From Kensington to Bow, from Camberwell to Somers Town, from Clapham to Deptford, the vast area of congested houses and tortuous streets was being swept continually. South of the Thames the loss of life was enormous, for thousands were unable to get beyond the zone of fire, and many in Brixton, Clapham, Camberwell, and Kennington were either maimed by flying fragments of shell, buried in the débris of their homes, or burned to death. The disasters wrought by the Frenchmen's improved long-range weapons were frightful.

London, the all-powerful metropolis, which had egotistically considered herself the impregnable Citadel of the World, fell to pieces and was consumed. She was frozen by terror, and lifeless. Her ancient monuments were swept away, her wealth melted in her coffers, her priceless objects of art were torn up and broken, and her streets ran with the blood of her starving toilers.

Day dawned grey, with stormlight gloom. Rain-clouds scudded swiftly across the leaden sky. Along the road in front of the Crystal Palace, where the French batteries were established, the deafening discharges that had continued incessantly during the night, and had smashed nearly all the glass in the sides and roof of the Palace, suddenly ceased.

The officers were holding a consultation over despatches received from the batteries at Tulse Hill, Streatham, Red Post Hill, One Tree Hill, and Greenwich, all of which stated that ammunition had run short, and they were therefore unable to continue the bombardment.

Neither of the ammunition trains of the two columns of the enemy had arrived, for, although the bombarding batteries were unaware of it, both had been captured and blown up by British Volunteers.

It was owing to this that the hostile guns were at last compelled to cease their thunder, and to this fact also was due the fortunes of the defenders in the events immediately following.

Our Volunteers occupying the line of defence north of London, through Epping and Brentwood to Tilbury, had for the past three weeks been in daily expectation of an attempt on the part of the invaders to land in Essex, and were amazed at witnessing this sudden bombardment. From their positions on the northern heights they could distinctly see how disastrous was the enemy's fire, and although they had been informed by telegraph of the reverses we had sustained at Guildford and Leatherhead, yet they had no idea that the actual attack on the metropolis would be made so swiftly. However, they lost not a moment. It was evident that the enemy had no intention of effecting a landing in Essex; therefore, with commendable promptitude, they decided to move across the Thames immediately, to reinforce their comrades in Surrey. Leaving the 2nd and 4th West Riding Artillery, under Col. Hoffmann and Col. N. Creswick, V.D., at Tilbury, and the Lincolnshire, Essex, and Worcestershire Volunteer Artillery, under Col. G. M. Hutton, V.D., Col. S. L. Howard, V.D., and Col. W. Ottley, the greater part of the Norfolk, Staffordshire, Tay, Aberdeen, Manchester, and Northern Counties Field Brigades moved south with all possible speed. From Brentwood, the 1st, 2nd, 3rd, and 4th Volunteer Battalions of the Norfolk Regiment, under Col. A. C. Dawson, Col. E. H. H. Combe, Col. H. E. Hyde,

V.D., and Col. C. W. J. Unthank, V.D.; the 1st and 2nd North Staffordshire, under Col. W. H. Dutton, V.D., and Col. F. D. Mort, V.D.; and the 1st, 2nd, and 3rd South Staffordshire, under Col. J. B. Cochrane, V.D., Col. T. T. Fisher, V.D., and Col. E. Nayler, V.D.; the 2nd, 4th, 5th, and 6th Royal Highlanders, under Col. W. A. Gordon, V.D., Col. Sir R. D. Moncreiffe, Col. Sir R. Menzies, V.D., and Col. Erskine; the 7th Argyll and Sutherland Highlanders, under Col. J. Porteous, V.D.; the 3rd, 4th, and 5th Gordon Highlanders, under Col. A. D. Fordyce, Col. G. Jackson, V.D., and Col. J. Johnston—were, as early as 2 a.m., on their way to London.

At this critical hour the Engineer and Railway Volunteer Staff Corps rendered invaluable services. Under the direction of Col. William Birt, trains held in readiness by the Great Eastern Railway brought the brigades rapidly to Liverpool Street, whence they marched by a circuitous route beyond the zone of fire by way of Marylebone, Paddington, Kensington Gardens, Walham Green, and across Wandsworth Bridge, thence to Upper Tooting, where they fell in with a large force of our Regular infantry and cavalry, who were on their way to outflank the enemy.

Attacking a detachment of the French at Tooting, they captured several guns, destroyed the enemy's field telegraph, and proceeded at once to Streatham, where the most desperate resistance was offered. A fierce fight occurred across Streatham Common, and over to Lower Norwood and Gipsy Hill, in which both sides lost very heavily. Nevertheless our Volunteers from Essex, although they had been on the march the greater part of the night, fought bravely, and inflicted terrible punishment upon their foe. The 3rd and 4th Volunteer Battalions of the Gordon Highlanders and the 1st Norfolk, attacking a French position near the mouth of the railway tunnel, displayed conspicuous bravery, and succeeded in completely annihilating their opponents; while in an opposite direction, towards Tooting, several troops of French cavalry were cut up and taken prisoners by two battalions of Royal Highlanders.

The batteries on Streatham Hill having been assaulted and taken, the force of defenders pushed quickly onward to Upper Norwood, where our cavalry, sweeping along Westow Hill and Church Street, fell upon the battery in front of the Crystal Palace. The enemy, owing to the interruption of their field telegraph, were unaware of their presence, and were completely surprised. Nevertheless French infantrymen rushed into the Crystal Palace Hotel, the White Swan, Stanton Harcourt, the Knoll, Rocklands, and other houses at both ends of the Parade, and from the windows poured forth withering volleys from their Lebels. Our cavalry, riding down at the broad Parade, used their sabres upon the artillerymen, and the whole of the French troops were quickly in a confused mass, unable to act with effect, and suffering appallingly from the steady fire of our Volunteers, who very soon cleared the enemy from the White Swan, and, having been drawn up outside, poured forth a galling rifle fire right along the enemy's position. Suddenly there was loud shouting, and the British 'Cease fire' sounded. The French, though fighting hard, were falling back gradually down the hill towards Sydenham Station, when suddenly shots were heard, and turbaned cavalry came riding into them at a terrific pace from the rear.

The British officers recognized the newcomers as a squadron of Bengal Lancers! At last India had sent us help, and our men sent up a loud cheer. A large force of cavalry and infantry, together with two regiments of Goorkas, had, it appeared, been landed at Sheerness. They had contemplated landing in Hampshire, but, more unfortunate than some of their compatriots who had effected a landing near Southampton, they were driven through the Straits of Dover by the enemy's cruisers. Marching north in company with a force from Chatham, they had earlier that morning attacked and routed the enemy's right flank at Blackheath, and, after capturing the battery of the foe at Greenwich, the greater part of the escort of which had been sent over to Lewisham an hour before, they slaughtered a battalion of Zouaves, and had then extended across to Denmark Hill, where a sanguinary struggle occurred.

The French on Dog Kennel, Red Post, Herne, and Tulse Hills turned their deadly machine guns upon them, and for a long time all the positions held out. At length, however, by reason of a splendid charge made by the Bengal Lancers, the battery at Red Post Hill was taken and the enemy slaughtered. During the next half-hour a fierce hand-to-hand struggle took place up Dog Kennel Hill from St Saviour's Infirmary, and presently, when the defenders gained the spur of the hill, they fought the enemy gallantly in Grove Lane, Private Road, Bromar Road, Camberwell Grove, and adjoining roads. Time after time the Indian cavalry charged, and the Goorkas, with their keen knives, hacked their way into those of the enemy who rallied. For nearly an hour the struggle continued desperately, showers of bullets from magazine rifles sweeping along the usually quiet suburban thoroughfares, until the roads were heaped with dead and dying, and the houses on either side bore evidence of the bloody fray. Then at last the guns placed along the hills all fell into our hands, and the French were almost completely swept out of existence.

Many were the terrible scenes witnessed in the gardens of the quaint last-century houses on Denmark Hill. Around those old-world residences, standing along the road leading down to Half Moon Lane, time-mellowed relics of an age bygone, Indians fought with Zouaves, and British Volunteers struggled fiercely hand to hand with French infantrymen. The quiet old-fashioned quarter, that was an aristocratic retreat when Camberwell was but a sylvan village with an old toll gate, when cows chewed the cud upon Walworth Common, and when the Walworth Road had not a house in the whole of it, was now the scene of a frightful massacre. The deafening explosions of cordite from magazine rifles, the exultant shouts of the victors and the hoarse shrieks of the dying, awakened the echoes in those quaint old gardens, with their Dutch-cut zigzag walks, enclosed by ancient red brick walls, moss-grown, lichen covered, and half hidden by ivy, honeysuckle, and creepers. Those spacious grounds, where men were now being mercilessly slaughtered, had been the scene of many a brilliant *fête champêtre*, where splendid satin-coated *beaux*, all smiles and *ailes de pigeon*, whispered scandal behind the fans of dainty dames in high-dressed wigs and patches, or, clad as Watteau shepherds, had danced the *al fresco* minuet with similarly attired shepherdesses, and later on played *piquet* and drank champagne till dawn.

In the good old Georgian days, when Johnson walked daily under the trees in Gough Square, when Macklin was playing the 'Man of the World', and when traitors heads blackened on Temple Bar, this colony was one of the must rural, exclusive, and gay in the vicinity of London. Alas, how it has decayed! Cheap 'desirable residences' have sprung up around it, the hand of the jerry-building Vandal has touched it, the sound of traffic roars about it; yet still there is a charm in those quaint old gardens of a forgotten era. From under the dark yew hedges the jonquils still peep out early—the flowers themselves are those old-fashioned sweet ones beloved of our grandmothers—and the tea roses still blossom on the crumbling walls and fill the air with their fragrance. But in this terrible struggle the walls were used as defences, the bushes were torn down and trampled under foot, and the flowers hung broken on their stalks, bespattered with men's blood!

Proceeding south again, the defenders successfully attacked the strong batteries on One Tree Hill at Honor Oak, and on Sydenham Hill and Forest Hill, and then extending across to the Crystal Palace, had joined hands with our Volunteers from Essex, where they were now wreaking vengeance for the ruthless destruction caused in London.

The bloodshed along the Crystal Palace Parade was fearful. The French infantry and artillery, overwhelmed by the onward rush of the defenders, and now under the British crossfire, fell in hundreds. Dark-faced Bengal Lancers and Goorkas, with British Hussars and Volunteers, descended upon them with appalling swiftness; and so complete was the slaughter, that of the whole force that had effected that terribly effectual bombardment from Sydenham, not more than a dozen survived.

By noon many of the shops on Westow Hill and private residences on College Hill and Sydenham Hill had been wantonly ignited by the enemy; but when the firing ceased some hours later, the roads were heaped with the corpses of those whose mission it had been to destroy London.

Of all those batteries which had caused such frightful desolation and loss of life during the night, not one now remained. The two French columns had been swiftly wiped out of existence; and although our forces had suffered very considerably, they nevertheless were able to go south to Croydon later that afternoon, in order to take part in resisting the vigorous and desperate attack which they knew would sooner or later be made by the whole French army massed beyond the Surrey Hills. The sun was on the horizon, and the shadows were already deepening.

Assistance had arrived tardily, for the damage to property in London during the night had been enormous; nevertheless at this the eleventh hour we had inflicted upon the French a crushing defeat, and now England waited, trembling and breathless, wondering what would be the final outcome of this fierce, bloody struggle for our national existence.

FIGHTING ON THE SURREY HILLS

Our valiant defenders were striking swift, decisive blows for England's honour. The French, demoralized by their severe defeat in the south of London, and suffering considerable loss in every other direction, fought desperately during the two days following the disastrous bombardment.

In darkness and sunlight fierce contests took place along the Surrey Hills, where our Volunteers, under Major-Gen. Lord Methuen, were still entrenched. Every copse bristled with rifles; red coats gleamed among the foliage, and winding highways were, alas! strewn with corpses. Guildford had again been reoccupied by our Regulars, who were reorganizing; and Leatherhead, holding out for another day, was retaken, after a terribly hard-fought battle, by the Highland, South of Scotland, and Glasgow Brigades, with the Ist Ayrshire and Galloway Artillery, under Col. J. G. Sturrock, V.D.; ist Lanarkshire, under Col. R. J. Bennett, V.D.; Ist Aberdeenshire, under Col. J. Ogston, V.D.; and ist North Riding Yorkshire Volunteer Artillery, under Major C. L. Bell. In such a splendid and gallant manner had our comparatively small force manoeuvred, that on the second night following the bombardment the whole of the invaders who had penetrated beyond our line of defence towards the metropolis had been completely wiped out, in addition to which the breach in our line had been filled up by strong reinforcements, and the enemy driven from the high ground between Box Hill and Guildford.

The invaders, finding how vigorously we repelled any attack, made terrific onslaughts on our position at various points they believed were vulnerable, but everywhere they were hurled back with appalling slaughter. Volunteers from Australia and the Cape, in addition to the other contingent of 10,000 Indian native troops, had been landed near Southampton, and had advanced to assist in this terrific struggle, upon the result of which the future of our Empire depended. Among these Colonials were 500 Victorian Rangers, 900 Victoria Mounted Rifles, and seven companies of Queensland Mounted Infantry, with two ambulance corps.

The Indians landed in splendid form, having brought their full war equipment with them without any contribution whatever from the Home Government, as it will be remembered they did when they landed at Malta during Lord Beaconsfield's administration. Having received intelligence of the movements of the two columns of the enemy that had gone to London after taking Leatherhead and Guildford, they pushed on to Petworth. By the time they arrived there, however, both towns had been recaptured by the British, who were then being severely harassed by the enemy massed along the south side of our defensive line. Although numerically inferior to the enemy occupying that part of the country, the Indians were already well accustomed to actual warfare, the majority having been engaged in operations against the hill tribes; therefore the commander decided to push on at once, and endeavour to outflank the large French force who with some Russian infantry had again attacked Guildford, and the manner in which this was accomplished was a single illustration of the valuable assistance the Indians rendered us in these days of bloodshed and despair.

One of the native officers of a Sikh regiment, the Subadar Banerji Singh, having served with Sir Peter Lumsden's expeditionary force some years before, had frequently come into contact with the Russians, and could speak Russian better than some of the soldiers of the Tsar's Asiatic corps. The commander of the Indian force, determined that his men should strike their blow and sustain their reputation, advanced with great caution from Petworth, and later in the afternoon of the second evening after the bombardment of London, two Sikhs scouting in front of the advance guard sighted a Russian bivouac on the road on the other side of the Wye Canal beyond Loxwood Bridge, which latter had been demolished. The Indians were thereupon halted on the road which runs through the wood near Plaistow, and the officers held council. Their information was unfortunately very meagre and their knowledge of the country necessarily vague; but the Subadar Banerji Singh, who was of unusually fair complexion, volunteered to don a Russian uniform, which had been taken with other property from a dead officer found upon the road and endeavour in that disguise to penetrate the enemy's lines.

Towards dusk he set out on his perilous journey, and, on arriving at the wrecked bridge, shouted over to two Russian sentries, explaining that he had been wounded and left behind after the fight at Haslemere, and requesting their assistance to enable him to cross. Believing him to be one of their infantry officers, they told him there were no means of crossing unless he could swim, as their engineers had sounded the canal before blowing up the bridge, and had found it twenty feet deep.

Banerji Singh questioned them artfully as to the position of their column, which they said intended, in co-operation with a great force of French cavalry and infantry, to again attack Guildford at dawn; and further, they told him in confidence that the rearguard to which they belonged only numbered about two thousand men, who had halted for the night with the transport waggons on the Guildford road, about two miles north of Alfold.

Then, after further confidences, they suggested that he should continue along the canal bank for about a mile and a half, where there was a bridge still intact, and near which he would find the rearguard.

Thanking them, he withdrew into the falling gloom, and a quarter of an hour later entered the presence of his commanding officer, who, of course, was delighted with the information thus elicited. The Subadar had carefully noted all the features of the canal bank and broken bridge, and the valuable knowledge he had obtained was at once put to account, and the General at once formed his force into two divisions. Then, after issuing instructions for the following day, he gave orders for a bivouac for the night.

The pioneers, however, were far from idle. During the night they worked with unflagging energy, quietly preparing a position for the guns to cover the contemplated passage at Loxwood Bridge, and before day broke the guns were mounted, and the Engineers were ready for action. As soon as there was sufficient light the laying of the pontoon commenced, but was at once noticed by the Russians, who opened fire, and very soon it was evident that information had been conveyed to the enemy's rearguard, and that they were returning to contest the passage.

In the meantime one division of the Indians, setting out before daybreak, had been cautiously working round to the main road crossing the canal north of Alfold, and succeeded in getting over soon after the majority of the Russian rearguard had left for the assistance of the detachment at Loxwood Bridge, and, after a sharp, decisive ngnt, succeeded in capturing the whole of the transport waggons. The Engineers, with the Indians, had in the meantime succeeded in completing their pontoon under cover of the guns, and the second division of the Indians, dark-faced, daring fellows, rushed across to the opposite bank, and descended upon the enemy with frightful effect. In the hot engagement that followed, the Russians, now attacked in both front and rear, were totally annihilated, and thus the whole of the reserve ammunition of the force assaulting Guildford fell into our hands.

This victory on the enemy's left flank caused the tide of events to turn in our favour, for the huge Russian and French columns that intended to again carry the hills from Dorking to Guildford were hampered by want of ammunition, and so vigorously did our Volunteers along the hills defend the repeated attacks, that the invaders were again driven back. Then, as they drew south to recover themselves, they were attacked on their left by a large body of our Regulars, and in the rear by the Indians and Australians. Over the country stretching across from Cranley through Ewhurst, Ockley, Capel, and Newdigate to Horley, the fighting spread, as each side struggled desperately for the mastery.

The fate of England, nay, of our vast British Empire, was in the hands of those of her stalwart sons of many races who were now wielding valiantly the rifle and the sword. Through that blazing September day, while the people of London wailed among the ruins of their homes, and, breathlessly anxious, awaited news of their victory or their doom, the whole of East Kent, the southern portion of Surrey and northern Sussex, became one huge battlefield. Of the vast bodies of troops massed over hill and dale every regiment became engaged.

The butchery was awful.

NAVAL BATTLE OFF DUNGENESS

On sea England was now showing the world how she still could fight. Following the desperate struggle off Sardinia, in which Italy had rendered us such valuable help, our Mediterranean Squadron attacked the French Fleet off Cape Tresforcas, on the coast of Morocco, and after a terrific battle, extending over two days, defeated them with heavy loss, several of the enemy's vessels being torpedoed and sunk, two of them rammed, and one so badly damaged that her captain ran her ashore on Alboran Island.

After this hard-earned victory, our Squadron passed out of the Mediterranean, and, returning home, had joined hands with the battered remnant of our Channel Fleet, now reinforced by several vessels recalled from foreign stations. Therefore, while the enemy marched upon London, we had collected our naval strength on the south coast, and at length made a final descent upon the enemy in British waters. The British vessels that passed Beachy Head coming up Channel on the night of the bombardment of London included the *Empress of India, Inflexible, Nile, Trafalgar, Magnificent, Hood, Warspite, Dreadnought, Camperdown, Blenheim, Barham, Benbow, Monarch, Anson, Immortalité,* and *Royal Sovereign*, with four of the new cruisers built under the Spencer programme, viz. the *Terrible, Powerful, Doris,* and *Isis,* and a number of smaller vessels, torpedo boats, and 'destroyers'.

At the same hour that our vessels were passing Beachy Head, the Coastguard at Sandwich Battery were suddenly alarmed by electric signals being flashed from a number of warships that were slowly passing the Gulf Stream revolving light towards the Downs. The sensation these lights caused among the Coastguard and Artillery was immediately dispelled when it was discovered that the warships were not hostile, but friendly; that the Kaiser had sent a German Squadron, in two divisions, to assist us, and that these vessels were on their way to unite with our own Fleet. The first division, it was ascertained, consisted of the *Baden*, flying the flag of Vice-Admiral Koester; the *Sachsen*, commanded by Prince Henry of Prussia; the *Württemberg*, and the *Bayern*— all of 7,400 tons, and each carrying 18 guns and nearly 400 men; while the despatch boat *Pfeil*, the new dynamite cruiser *Trier*, and a number of torpedo boats, accompanied them. The second division, under Rear-Admiral von Diederichs on board the *König Wilhelm*, consisted of the *Brandenburg, Kurfürst Friedrich Wilhelm*, and *Wœrth*, each of 10,300 tons, and carrying 32 guns; the *Deutschland* and the *Friedrich der Grosse*, with the despatch vessel *Wacht*, and several torpedo gunboats and other craft.

Before dawn, the British and German Fleets united near South Sand Head light, off the South Foreland, and it was decided to commence the attack without delay. Turning west again, the British ships, accompanied by those of the Emperor William, proceeded slowly down Channel in search of the enemy, which they were informed by signal had been sighted by the Coastguard at East Wear, near Folkestone, earlier in the night. Just as day broke, however, when the defenders were opposite Dymchurch, about eight miles from the land, the enemy were discovered in force. Apparently the French and Russian Fleets had combined, and were preparing for a final descent upon Dover, or an assault upon the Thames defences; and it could be seen that, with both forces so strong, the fight would inevitably be one to the death.

Little time was occupied in preliminaries. Soon our ships were within range in fighting formation in single column in line abreast, while the French, under Admiral le Bourgeois, advanced in single column in line ahead. The French flagship, leading, was within 2,000 yards of the British line, and had not disclosed the nature of her attack. The enemy's Admiral had signalled to the ships astern of him to follow his motions together, as nearly as possible to concentrate their guns at point blank, right ahead, and to pour their shot on the instant of passing our ships. He had but three minutes to decide upon the attack, and as he apparently elected to pierce the centre of our line, the British had no time to counteract him. The French Admiral therefore continued his course, and as he passed between the *Camperdown* and *Blenheim*, he discharged his guns, receiving the British broadsides and bow fire at the same time. In a few minutes, however, it was seen that the French attack had been frustrated, and as dawn spread the fighting increased, and the lines became broken. The ponderous guns of the battleships thundered, and ere long the whole of the great naval force was engaged in this final struggle for England's freedom. The three powerful French battleships, *Jauréguiberry, Jemappes*, and *Dévastation*, and the submarine torpedo boat *Gustave Zédé*, fiercely attacked the *Brandenburg* and the *König Wilhelm*; while the *Camperdown, Anson, Dreadnought*, and *Warspite* fought desperately with half a dozen of the enemy's battleships, all of which suffered considerably. Our torpedo boats, darting swiftly hither and thither, performed much effective service, and many smart manoeuvres were carried out by astute officers in command of those wasps of the sea. In one instance a torpedo boat, which had designs upon a Russian ironclad, obtained cover by sending in front of her a gunboat which emitted an immense quantity of dense smoke. This of course obscured from view the torpedo boat under the gunboat's stern, and those on board the Tsar's battleship pounded away at the gunboat, unconscious of the presence of the dangerous little craft. Just as the gunboat got level with the battleship, however, the torpedo boat emerged from the cloud of smoke, and, darting along, ejected its Whitehead with such precision that five minutes later the Russian leviathan sank beneath the dark green waters. Almost at the same moment, the new German dynamite cruiser destroyed a French cruiser, and a fierce and sanguinary encounter took place between the *Immortalité* and the *Tréhouart*. The former's pair of 22-tonners, in combination with her ten 6-inch guns, wrought awful havoc on board the French vessel; nevertheless, from the turret of her opponent there came a deadly fire which spread death and destruction through the ship. Suddenly the Frenchman swung round, and with her quick-firing guns shedding a deadly storm of projectiles, came full upon the British vessel. The impact and the angle at which she was struck was not, however, sufficient to ram her, consequently the two vessels became entangled, and amid the rain of bullets the Frenchmen made a desperate attempt to board our ship. A few who managed to spring upon the *Immortalité*'s deck were cut down instantly, but a couple of hundred fully armed men were preparing to make a rush to overpower our bluejackets. On board the British cruiser, however, the enemy's intentions had been divined, and certain precautions taken. The *Fusiliers Marins*, armed with

Lebels and cutlasses, suddenly made a desperate, headlong rush upon the British cruiser's deck, but just as fifty of them gained their goal, a great hose attached to one of the boilers was brought into play, and scalding water poured upon the enemy. This, in addition to some hand charges at that moment thrown, proved successful in repelling the attack; but just as the survivors retreated in disorder there was a dull explosion, and then it was evident, from the confusion on board the French ship, that she had been torpedoed by a German boat, and was sinking.

Humanely, our vessel, the *Immortalité*, rescued the whole of her opponent's men ere she sank; but it was found that in the engagement her captain and half her crew had been killed. On every hand the fight continued with unabated fierceness; every gun was worked to its utmost capacity, and amid the smoke and din every vessel was swept from stem to stern. As morning wore on, the enemy met with one or two successes. Our two new cruisers *Terrible* and *Powerful* had been sunk by French torpedoes; the *Hood* had been rammed by the *Amiral Baudin*, and gone to the bottom with nearly every soul on board; while the German despatch boat *Wacht* had been captured, and seven of our torpedo boats had been destroyed. During the progress of the fight, the vessels came gradually nearer Dungeness, and at eleven o'clock they were still firing at each other, with appalling results on either side.

At such close quarters did this great battle occur, that the loss of life was awful, and throughout the ships the destruction was widespread and frightful. About noon the enemy experienced two reverses. The French battleship *Formidable* blew up with a terrific report, filling the air with débris, her magazine having exploded; while just at that moment the *Courbet*, whose 48-tonners had caused serious damage to the *Warspite*, was suddenly rammed and sunk by the *Empress of India*.

This, the decisive battle, was the most vigorously contested naval fight during the whole of the hostilities. The scene was terrible. The steel leviathans of the sea were being rent asunder and pulverized by the terribly destructive modern arms, and amid the roar and crashing of the guns, shells were bursting everywhere, carrying away funnels, fighting tops, and superstructures, and wrecking the crowded spaces between the decks. Turrets and barbettes were torn away, guns dismounted by the enormous shells from heavy guns; steel armour was torn up and thrown aside like paper, and many shots entering broadsides, passed clean through and out at the other side. Whitehead torpedoes, carrying heavy charges of gun-cotton, exploded now and then under the enemy's ships; while both British and French torpedo boat 'destroyers', running at the speed of an ordinary train, were sinking or capturing where they could.

Through the dull, gloomy afternoon the battle continued. Time after time our ships met with serious reverses, for the *Anson* was sunk by the Russian flagship *Alexander II*, assisted by two French cruisers, and this catastrophe was followed almost immediately by the torpedoing of the new British cruiser *Doris*, and the capture of the new German dynamite cruiser *Trier*.

By this time, however, the vessels had approached within three miles of Dungeness, and the *Camperdown, Empress of India, Royal Sovereign, Inflexible*, and *Warspite*, lying near one another, fought nine of the enemy's vessels, inflicting upon them terrible punishment. Shots from the 67-tonners of the *Empress of India, Royal Sovereign*, and *Camperdown*, combined with those from the 22-tonners of the *Warspite*, swept the enemy's vessels with devastating effect, and during the three-quarters of an hour that the fight between these vessels lasted, the scene of destruction was appalling. Suddenly, with a brilliant flash and deafening detonation, the Russian flagship *Alexander II*, one of the vessels now engaging the five British ships, blew up and sank, and ere the enemy could recover from the surprise this disaster caused them, the *Camperdown* rammed the *Amiral Baudin*, while the *Warspite* sank the French cruiser *Cécille*, the submarine boat *Gustave Zédé*, and afterwards captured the torpedo gunboat *Bombe*.

This rapid series of terrible disasters apparently demoralized the enemy. They fought recklessly, and amid the din and confusion two Russian vessels collided, and were so seriously damaged that both settled down, their crews being rescued by British torpedo boats. Immediately afterwards, however, a frightful explosion rent the air with a deafening sound that dwarfed into insignificance the roar of the heavy guns, and the French battleship *Jaur'guiberry* was completely broken into fragments, scarcely any of her hull remaining. The enemy were amazed. A few moments later another explosion occurred, even louder than the first. For a second the French battleship *D'vastation*, which had been engaging the *Royal Sovereign*, was obscured by a brilliant flash, then, as fragments of steel and human limbs were precipitated on every side, it was seen that that vessel also had been completely blown out of the water!

The enemy stood appalled. The defenders themselves were at first dumbfounded. A few moments later, however, it became known throughout the British ships that the battery at Dungeness, two miles and a half distant, were rendering assistance with the new pneumatic gun, the secret of which the Government had guarded so long and so well. Five years before, this frightfully deadly weapon had been tested, and proved so successful that the one gun made was broken up and the plans preserved with the utmost secrecy in a safe at the War Office. Now, however, several of the weapons had been constructed, and one of them had been placed in the battery at Dungeness. The British vessels drew off to watch the awful effect of the fire from these marvellous and terribly destructive engines of modern warfare. The enemy would not surrender, so time after time deafening explosions sounded, and time after time the hostile ships were shattered into fragments.

Each shot fired by this new pneumatic gun contained 900 lbs of dynamite, which could strike effectively at four miles! The result of such a charge exploding on a ship was appalling; the force was terrific, and could not be withstood by the strongest vessel ever constructed. Indeed, the great armoured vessels were being pulverized as easily as glass balls struck by bullets, and every moment hundreds of poor fellows were being hurled into eternity. At last the enemy discovered the distant source of the fire, and prepared to escape beyond range; but in this they were unsuccessful, for, after a renewed and terrific fight, in which three French ironclads were sunk and two of our cruisers were torpedoed, our force and our allies the Germans succeeded in capturing the remainder of the hostile ships and torpedo boats.

The struggle had been frightful; but the victory was magnificent.

That same night the British ships steamed along the Sussex

coast and captured the whole of the French and Russian transports, the majority of which were British vessels that had been seized while lying in French and Russian ports at the time war was declared. The vessels were lying between Beachy Head and Selsey Bill, and by their capture the enemy's means of retreat were at once totally cut off.

Thus, at the eleventh hour, the British Navy had shown itself worthy of its reputation, and England regained the supremacy of the seas.

THE DAY OF RECKONING

The Day of Reckoning dawned.

On land the battle was terrific; the struggle was the most fierce and bloody of any during the invasion. The British Regulars holding the high ground along from Crowborough to Ticehurst, and from Etchingham, through Brightling and Ashburnham, down to Battle, advanced in a huge fighting line upon the enemy's base around Eastbourne. The onslaught was vigorously repelled, and the battle across the Sussex Downs quickly became a most wild and sanguinary one; but as the day passed, although the defenders were numerically very weak, they nevertheless gradually effected terrible slaughter, capturing the whole of the enemy's stores, and taking nearly five thousand prisoners.

In Kent the French had advanced from East Grinstead through Edenbridge, extending along the hills south of Westerham, and in consequence of these rapid successes the depot of stores and ammunition which had been maintained at Sevenoaks was being removed to Bromley by rail; but as the officer commanding the British troops at Eynsford could see that it would most probably be impossible to get them all away before Sevenoaks was attacked, orders were issued that at a certain hour the remainder should be destroyed. The force covering the removal only consisted of two battalions of the Duke of Cambridge's Own (Middlesex) Regiment and half a squadron of the 9th Lancers; but the hills north of Sevenoaks from Luddesdown through Stanstead, Otford, Shoreham, Halstead, Farnborough, and Keston were still held by our Volunteers. These infantry battalions included the ist and 2nd Derbyshire Regiment (Sherwood Foresters), under Col. A. Buchanan, V.D., and Col. E. Hall, V.D.; the Ist Nottinghamshire, under Col. A. Cantrell-Hubbersty; the 4th Derbyshire, under Lord Newark; the ist and 2nd Lincolnshire, under Col. J. G. Williams, V.D., and Col. R. G. Ellison; the ist Leicestershire, under Col. S. Davis, V.D.; the ist Northamptonshire, under Col. T.J. Walker, V.D.; the ist and 2nd Shropshire Light Infantry, under Col. J. A. Anstice, V.D., and Col. R. T. Masefield; the ist Herefordshire, under Col. T. H. Purser, V.D.; the ist, 3rd, and 4th South Wales Borderers, under Col. T. Wood, Col. J. A. Bradney, and Col. H. Burton, V.D.; the ist and 2nd Warwickshire, under Col. W. S. Jervis and Col. L. V. Loyd; the Ist and 2nd Welsh Fusiliers, under Col. C. S. Mainwaring and Col. B. G. D. Cooke, V.D.; the 2nd Welsh Regiment, under Col. A. P. Vivian, V.D.; the 3rd Glamorganshire, under Col. J. C. Richardson, V.D.; and the ist Worcestershire, under Col. W. H. Talbot, V.D.; while the artillery consisted of the 3rd Kent, under Col. Hozier; the ist Monmouthshire, under

Col. C. T. Wallis; the 1st Shropshire and Staffordshire, under Col. J. Strick, V.D.; and the 5th Lancashire, under Col. W. H. Hunt.

The events which occurred outside Sevenoaks are perhaps best described by Capt. A. E. Brown, of the 4th V.B. West Surrey Regiment, who was acting as one of the special correspondents of the *Standard*. He wrote:

'I was in command of a piquet consisting of fifty men of my regiment at Turvan's Farm, and about three hours before the time to destroy the remainder of the stores at Sevenoaks my sentries were suddenly driven in by the enemy, who were advancing from the direction of Froghall. As I had orders to hold the farm at any cost, we immediately prepared for action. Fortunately we had a fair supply of provisions and plenty of ammunition, for since War had broken out the place had been utilized as a kind of outlying fort, although at this time only my force occupied it. Our equipment included two machine guns, and it was mainly by the aid of these we were saved.

'The strength of the attacking force appeared to be about four battalions of French infantry and a battalion of Zouaves, with two squadrons of Cuirassiers. Their intention was, no doubt, to cut the railway line near Twitton, and thus prevent the removal of the Sevenoaks stores. As soon as the cavalry scouts came within range we gave them a few sharp volleys, and those who were able immediately retired in disorder. Soon afterwards, however, the farm was surrounded, but I had previously sent information to our reserves, and suggested that a sharp watch should be kept upon the line from Twitton to Sevenoaks, for of course I could do nothing with my small force. Dusk was now creeping on, and as the enemy remained quiet for a short time it seemed as though they intended to assault our position when it grew dark.

'Before night set in, however, my messenger, who had managed to elude the vigilance of the enemy, returned, with a letter from a brother officer stating that a great naval battle had been fought in the Channel; and further, that the enemy's retreat had been cut off, and that the Kentish defenders had already retaken the invaders' base at Eastbourne. If we could, therefore, still hold the Surrey Hills, there was yet a chance of thoroughly defeating the French and Russians, even though one strong body was reported as having taken Guildford and Leatherhead, and was now marching upon London.

'As evening drew on we could hear heavy firing in the direction of Sevenoaks, but as we also heard a train running it became evident that we still held the station. Nevertheless, soon after dark there was a brilliant flash which for a second lit up the country around like day, and a terrific report followed. We knew the remainder of our stores and ammunition had been demolished in order that it should not fall into the enemy's hands!

'Shortly afterwards we were vigorously attacked, and our position quickly became almost untenable by the dozens of bullets projected in every direction where the flash of our rifles could be seen. Very soon some of the farm outbuildings fell into the hands of the Frenchmen, and they set them on fire, together with a number of haystacks, in order to burn us out. This move, however, proved pretty disastrous to them, for the leaping flames quickly rendered it light as day, and showed them up, while at the same time flashes from our muzzles were almost invisible to them. Thus we were enabled to bring our two machine guns into action, and break up every party of Frenchmen who showed themselves. Away over Sevenoaks there was a glare in the sky, for the enemy were looting and burning the town. Meanwhile, however, our men who had been defending the place had retreated to Dunton Green after blowing up the stores, and there they reformed and were quickly moving off in the direction of Twitton. Fortunately they had heard the commencement of the attack on us, and the commander, halting his force, had sent out scouts towards Chevening, and it appeared they reached us just at the moment the enemy had fired the stacks. They worked splendidly, and, after going nearly all round the enemy's position, returned and reported to their Colonel, who at once resolved to relieve us.

'As may be imagined, we were in a most critical position by this time, especially as we were unaware that assistance was so near. We had been ordered to hold the farm, and we meant to do it as long as breath remained in our bodies. All my men worked magnificently, and displayed remarkable coolness, even at the moment when death stared us in the face. The reports of the scouts enabled their Colonel to make his disposition very carefully, and it was not long before the enemy were almost completely surrounded. We afterwards learnt that our reserves at Stockholm Wood had sent out a battalion, which fortunately came in touch with the survivors of the Sevenoaks force just as they opened a desperate onslaught upon the enemy.

'With the fierce flames and blinding smoke from the burning stacks belching in our faces, we fought on with fire around us on every side. As the fire drew nearer to us the heat became intense, the showers of sparks galled us almost as much as the enemy's bullets, and some of us had our eyebrows and hair singed by the fierce flames. Indeed, it was as much as we could do to keep our ammunition from exploding; nevertheless we kept up our stream of lead, pouring volley after volley upon those who had attacked us. Nevertheless, with such a barrier of flame and obscuring smoke between us we could see but little in the darkness beyond, and we all knew that if we emerged from cover we should be picked off easily and not a man would survive. The odds were against us. More than twenty of my brave fellows had fired their last shot, and now lay with their dead upturned faces looking ghastly in the brilliant glare, while a number of others had sunk back wounded. The heat was frightful, the smoke stifling, and I had just given up all hope of relief, and had set my teeth, determined to die like an Englishman should, when we heard a terrific volley of musketry at close quarters, and immediately afterwards a dozen British bugles sounded the charge. The scene of carnage that followed was terrible. Our comrades gave one volley from their magazine rifles, and then charged with the bayonet, taking the enemy completely by surprise.

'The Frenchmen tried to rally, but in vain, and among those huge burning barns and blazing ricks they all fell or were captured. Dozens of them struggled valiantly till the last; but, refusing to surrender, they were slaughtered amid a most frightful scene of blood and fire. The events of that night were horrible, and the true extent of the losses on both sides was only revealed when the flames died down and the parting clouds above heralded another grey and toilsome day.'

Late on the previous evening the advance guard of the enemy proceeding north towards Caterham came in touch with the defenders north of Godstone. The French cavalry had seized Red Hill Junction Station at sundown, and some of their scouts suddenly came upon a detached post of the 17th Middlesex Volunteers at Tyler's Green, close to Godstone. A very sharp skirmish ensued, but the Volunteers, although suffering severe losses, held their own, and the cavalry went off along the Oxted Road. This being reported to the British General, special orders were at once sent to Col. Trotter, the commander of this section of the outpost line.

From the reports of the inhabitants and of scouts sent out in plain clothes, it was believed that the French intended massing near Tandridge, and that they would therefore wait for supports before attempting to break through our outpost line, which still remained intact from the high ground east of Leatherhead to the hills north of Sevenoaks. During the night Oxted and Godstone were occupied by the enemy, and early in the morning their advance guard, consisting of four battalions of infantry, a squadron of cavalry, a battalion of Zouaves, and a section of field artillery, proceeded north in two columns, one along the Roman road leading past Rook's Nest, and the other past Flinthall Farm.

At the latter place the sentries of the 17th Middlesex fell back upon their piquets, and both columns of the enemy came into action simultaneously. The French infantry on the high road soon succeeded in driving back the Volunteer piquet upon the supports, under Lieut. Michaelis, stationed at the junction of the Roman road with that leading to Godstone Quarry. A strong barricade with two deep trenches in front had here been constructed, and as soon as the survivors of the piquet got under cover, two of the defenders' machine guns opened fire from behind the barricade, assisted at the same moment by a battery on Gravelly Hill.

The French artillery had gone on towards Flinthall Farm, but in passing the north edge of Rook's Nest Park their horses were shot by some Inniskilling Fusiliers lying in ambush, and by these two reverses, combined with the deadly fire from the two machine guns at the farm, the column was very quickly thrown into confusion. It was then decided to make a counter-attack, and the available companies at this section of the outpost line, under Col. Brown and Col. Roche, succeeded, after nearly two hours' hard fighting, in retaking Godstone and Oxted, compelling the few survivors of the enemy's advance guard to fall back to Blindley Heath.

In the meantime our troops occupying the line from Halstead to Chatham and Maidstone went down into battle, attacking the French right wing at the same time as the Indians were attacking their left, while the Volunteers from the Surrey Hills engaged the main body. The day was blazing hot, the roads dusty, and there was scarce a breath of wind. So hot, indeed, was it, that many on both sides fell from hunger, thirst, and sheer starvation. Yet, although the force of the invaders was nearly twice the numerical strength of the defenders, the latter fought on with undaunted courage, striking their swift, decisive blows for England and their Queen.

The enemy, now driven into a triangle, fought with demoniacal strength, and that frenzied courage begotten of despair. On the hills around Sevenoaks and across to the valley at Otford, the slaughter of the French was fearful. Britons fighting for their homes and their country were determined that Britannia should still be Ruler of the World.

From Wimlet Hill the enemy were by noon totally cut up and routed by the 12th Middlesex (Civil Service), under Lord Bury; the 25th (Bank), under Capt. W. J. Coe, V.D.; the 13th (Queen's), under Col. J.W. Comerford; the 21st Middlesex, under Col. H. B. Deane, V.D.; and the 22nd, under Col. W. J. Alt, V.D. Over at Oxted, however, they rallied, and some brilliant charges by Cossacks, the slaughter of a portion of our advance guard, and the capture of one of our Volunteer batteries on Botley Hill, checked our advance.

The French, finding their right flank being so terribly cut up, had suddenly altered their tactics, and were now concentrating their forces upon the Volunteer position at Caterham in an endeavour to break through our defensive line.

But the hills about that position held by the North

London, West London, South London, Surrey, and Cheshire Brigades were well defended, and the General had his finger upon the pulse of his command. Most of the positions had been excellently chosen. Strong batteries were established at Gravelly Hill by the 9th Lancashire Volunteer Artillery, under Col. F. Ainsworth, V.D.; at Harestone Farm by the 1st Cinque Ports, under Col. P.S. Court, V.D.; at White Hill by the 1st Northumberland and the 1st Norfolk, under Col. P.Watts and Col. T.Wilson, V.D.; at Botley Hill by the 6th Lancashire, under Col. H. J. Robinson, V.D.; at Tandridge Hill by the 3rd Lancashire, under Col. R. W. Thom, V.D.; at Chaldon by the 1st Newcastle, under Col. W. M. Angus, V.D., who had come south after the victory at the Tyneside; at Warlingham village by the 1st Cheshire, commanded by Col. H. T. Brown, V.D.; at Warlingham Court by the 2nd Durham, under Col. J. B. Eminson, V.D.; on the Sanderstead road, near King's Wood, by the 2nd Cinque Ports, under Col. W. Taylor, V.D.; and on the railway near Woldingham the 1st Sussex had stationed their armoured train with 40-pounder breech-loading Armstrongs, which they fired very effectively from the permanent way.

Through Limpsfield, Oxted, Godstone, Bletchingley, and Nutsfield, towards Reigate, Frenchmen and Britons fought almost hand to hand. The defenders suffered severely, owing to the repeated charges of the French Dragoons along the highway between Oxted and Godstone, nevertheless the batteries of the 6th Lancashire on Tandridge Hill, which commanded a wide area of country occupied by the enemy, wrought frightful execution in their ranks. In this they were assisted by the 17th Middlesex, under Col. W. J. Brown, V.D., who with four Maxims at one period of the fight surprised and practically annihilated a whole battalion of French infantry. But into this attack on Caterham the enemy put his whole strength, and from noon until four o'clock the fighting along the valley was a fierce combat to the death.

With every bit of cover bristling with magazine rifles, and every available artillery position shedding forth a storm of bullets and shell, the loss of life was awful. Invaders and defenders fell in hundreds, and with burning brow and dry parched throat expired in agony. The London Irish, under Col. J. Ward, V.D.; the Post Office Corps, under Col. J. Du Plat Taylor, V.D., and Col. S. R. Thompson, V.D.; the Inns of Court, under Col. C. H. Russell, V.D.; and the Cyclists, led by Major T. De B. Holmes, performed many gallant deeds, and served their country well. The long, dusty highways were quickly covered with the bodies of the unfortunate victims, who lay with blanched, bloodless faces and sightless eyes turned upward to the burning sun. On over them rode madly French cavalry and Cossacks, cutting their way into the British infantry, never to return.

Just, however, as they prepared for another terrific onslaught, the guns of the ist Cheshire battery at Warlingham village thundered, and with smart section volleys added by detachments of the London Scottish, under Major W. Brodie, V.D., and the Artists, under Capt. W. L. Duffield and Lieut. Pott, the road was in a few minutes strewn with horses and men dead and dying.

Still onward there rushed along the valley great masses of French infantry, but the 1st, 2nd, and 3rd Volunteer Battalions of the Royal Fusiliers, under Col. G. C. Clark, V.D;, Col. A. L. Keller, and Col. L. Whewell respectively; the 2nd V. B. Middlesex Regiment, under Col. G. Brodie Clark, V.D.; the 3rd Middlesex, under Col. R. Hennell, D.S.O., late of the Indian Army; and the ist, 2nd, 3rd, and 4th West Surrey, under Col. J. Freeland, V.D., Col. G. Drewitt, V.D., Col. S. B. Bevington, V.D., and Col. F. W. Haddan, V.D., engaged them, and by dint of desperate effort, losing heavily all the time, they defeated them, drove them back, and slaughtered them in a manner that to a non-combatant was horrible and appalling. Time after time, the enemy, still being harassed by the British Regulars on their right, charged up the valley, in order to take the battery at Harestone Farm; but on each occasion few of those who dashed forward survived. The dusty roads, the grassy slopes, and the ploughed lands were covered with corpses, and blood draining into the springs and rivulets tinged their crystal waters.

As afternoon passed and the battle continued, it was by no means certain that success in this fierce final struggle would lie with us. Having regard to the enormous body of invaders now concentrated on the Surrey border, and striving by every device to force a passage through our lines, our forces, spread over such a wide area and outflanking them, were necessarily weak. It was therefore only by the excellent tactics displayed by our officers, and the magnificent courage of the men themselves, that we had been enabled to hold back these overwhelming masses, which had already desolated Sussex with fire and sword.

Our Regulars operating along the old Roman highway through Blindley Heath—where the invaders were making a desperate stand—and over to Lingfield, succeeded, after very hard fighting, in clearing the enemy off the railway embankment from Crowhurst along to South Park Farm, and following them up, annihilated them.

Gradually, just at sundown, a strong division of the enemy were outflanked at Godstone, and, refusing to lay down their arms, were simply swept out of existence, scarcely a single man escaping. Thus forced back from, perhaps, the most vulnerable point in our defences, the main body of the enemy were then driven away upon Redhill, still fighting fiercely. Over Redstone Hill, through Mead Vale, and across Reigate Park to the Heath, the enemy were shot down in hundreds by our Regulars; while our Volunteers, whose courage never deserted them, engaged the French in hand-to-hand encounters through the streets of Redhill and Reigate, as far as Underhill Park.

In Hartswood a company of the 4th East Surrey Rifles, under Major S. B. Wheaton, V.D., were lying in ambush, when suddenly among the trees they caught glimpses of red, baggy trousers, and scarlet, black-tasselled fezes, and a few seconds later they found that a large force of Zouaves were working through the wood. A few moments elapsed, and the combat commenced. The Algerians fought like demons, and with bullet and bayonet inflicted terrible punishment upon us; but as they emerged into the road preparatory to firing a volley into the thickets, they were surprised by a company of the 2nd Volunteer Battalion of the East Surrey Regiment, under Capt. Pott, who killed and wounded half their number, and took the remainder prisoners.

Gradually our Volunteer brigades occupying the long range of hills united with our Regulars still on the enemy's right from Reigate to Crawley, and closed down upon the foe, slowly narrowing the sphere of their operations, and by degrees forcing them back due westward. Russians and French, who had attacked Dorking, had by this time been defeated with heavy loss, and by dusk the main body had been thrown back to Newdigate, where in Reffold's Copse one or two very sanguinary encounters occurred. These, however, were not always in our favour, for the Civil Service Volunteers here sustained very heavy losses. On the railway embankment, and on the road running along the crest of the hill to Dorking, the French made a stand, and there wrought frightful execution among our men with their machine guns. Around Beare Green, Trout's Farm, and behind the 'White Hart' at Holmwood, the enemy rapidly brought their guns into play, and occupied such strong strategic positions that as night drew on it became evident that they intended to remain there until the morrow.

The defenders had but little cover, and consequently felt the withering fire of the French very severely. The latter had entrenched themselves, and now in the darkness it was difficult for our men to discern their exact position. Indeed, the situation of our forces became very serious and unsafe as night proceeded; but at length, about ten o'clock, a strong force of British Regulars, including the Sikhs and a detachment of Australians, swept along the road from Dorking, and came suddenly upon the French patrols. These were slaughtered with little resistance, and almost before the enemy were aware of it, the whole position was completely surrounded.

Our men then used their field searchlights with very

great advantage; for, as the enemy were driven out into the open, they were blinded by the glare, and fell an easy prey to British rifles; while the Frenchmen's own machine guns were turned upon them with frightful effect, their battalions being literally mowed down by the awful hail of bullets.

'FOR ENGLAND!'

Through the whole night the battle still raged furiously. The enemy fought on with reckless, unparalleled daring. Chasseurs and Zouaves, Cuirassiers, Dragoons, and infantry from the Loire and the Rhone struggled desperately, contesting every step, and confident of ultimate victory.

But the enemy had at last, by the splendid tactics of the defenders, been forced into a gradually contracting square, bounded by Dorking and Guildford in the north, and Horsham and Billinghurst in the south, and soon after midnight, with a concentric movement from each of the four corners, British Regulars and Volunteers advanced steadily upon the foe, surrounding and slaughtering them.

The horrors of that night were frightful; the loss of life on every hand enormous. Britannia had husbanded her full strength until this critical moment; for now, when the fate of her Empire hung upon a single thread, she sent forth her valiant sons, who fell upon those who had desecrated and destroyed their homes, and wreaked a terrible vengeance.

Through the dark, sultry hours this awful destruction of life continued with unabated fury, and many a Briton closed with his foe in death embrace, or fell forward mortally wounded. Of British heroes there were many that night, for true pluck showed itself everywhere, and Englishmen performed many deeds worthy of their traditions as the most courageous and undaunted among nations.

Although the French Commander-in-Chief had been killed, yet the enemy still fought on tenaciously, holding their ground on Leith Hill and through Pasture Wood to Wotton and Abinger, until at length, when the saffron streak in the sky heralded another blazing day, the straggling, exhausted remnant of the once-powerful legions of France and Russia, perspiring, dust-covered, and blood-stained, finding they stood alone, and that the whole of Sussex and Surrey had been swept and their comrades slaughtered, laid down their arms and eventually surrendered.

After these three breathless days of butchery and bloodshed England was at last victorious!

In this final struggle for Britain's freedom the invader had been crushed and his power broken; for, thanks to our gallant citizen soldiers, the enemy that had for weeks overrun our smiling land like packs of hungry wolves, wantonly burning our homes and massacring the innocent and unprotected, had at length met with their well-merited deserts, and now lay spread over the miles of pastures, cornfields, and forests, stark, cold, and dead.

Britain had at last vanquished the two powerful nations that had sought by ingenious conspiracy to accomplish her downfall.

Thousands of her brave sons had, alas! fallen while fighting under the British flag. Many of the principal streets of her gigantic capital were only parallel lines of gaunt, blackened ruins, and many of her finest cities lay wrecked, shattered, and desolate; yet this terrible ordeal had happily not weakened her power one iota, nor had she been ousted from her proud position as chief among the mighty Empires of the world.

Three days after the great and decisive battle of Caterham, the British troops, with their compatriots from the Cape, Australia, Canada, and India, entered London triumphantly, bringing with them some thousands of French and Russian prisoners. In the streets, as, ragged and dusty, Britain's defenders passed through on their way to a great Open-Air Thanksgiving Service in Hyde Park, there were scenes of the wildest enthusiasm. With heartfelt gratitude, the people, scrambling over the débris heaped each side of the streets, cheered themselves hoarse; the men grasping the hands of Volunteers and veterans, and the women, weeping for joy, raising the soldiers' hands to their lips. The glad tidings of victory caused rejoicings everywhere. England, feeling herself free, breathed again. In every church and chapel through the United Kingdom special Services of Thanksgiving for deliverance from the invaders' thrall were held, while in every town popular fetes were organized, and delighted Britons gaily celebrated their magnificent and overwhelming triumph.

In this disastrous struggle between nations France had suffered frightfully. Paris, bombarded and burning, capitulated on the day following the battle of Caterham, and the legions of the Kaiser marched up the Boulevards with their brilliant cavalry uniforms flashing in the sun. Over the Hotel de Ville, the Government buildings on the Quai d'Orsay, and the Ministries of War and Marine, the German flag was hoisted, and waved lazily in the autumn breeze, while the Emperor William himself had an interview with the French President at the Elysée.

That evening all France knew that Paris had fallen. In a few days England was already shipping back to Dieppe and Riga her prisoners of war, and negotiations for peace had commenced. As security against any further attempts on England, Italian troops were occupying the whole of Southern France from Grenoble to Bordeaux; and the Germans, in addition to occupying Paris, had established their headquarters in Moghilev, and driven back the Army of the Tsar far beyond the Dnieper.

From both France and Russia, Germany demanded huge indemnities, as well as a large tract of territory in Poland, and the whole of the vast Champagne country from Givet, on the Belgian frontier, down to the Sâone.

Ten days later France was forced to accept the preliminaries of a treaty which we proposed. This included the cession to us of Algiers, with its docks and harbour, so that we might establish another naval station in the Mediterranean, and the payment of an indemnity of £250,000,000. Our demands upon Russia at the same time were that she should withdraw all her troops from Bokhara, and should cede to us the whole of that portion of the Trans-Caspian territory lying between the mouths of the Oxus and Kizil Arvat, thence along the Persian frontier to Zulfikai, along the Afghan frontier to Karki, and from there up the bank of the Oxus to the Aral Sea. This vast area of land included the cities of Khiva and Merv, the many towns around Kara Khum, the country of the Kara Turkomans, the Tekeh and the Yomuts, and the annexation of it by Britain would effectually prevent the Russians ever advancing upon India.

Upon these huge demands, in addition to the smaller ones by Italy and Austria, a Peace Conference was opened at Brussels without delay, and at length France and her Muscovite ally, both vanquished and ruined, were compelled to accept the proposals of Britain and Germany.

Hence, on November 16th, 1897, the Treaty of Peace was signed, and eight days later was ratified. Then the huge forces of the Kaiser gradually withdrew into Germany, and the soldiers of King Humbert recrossed the Alps, while we shipped back the remainder of our prisoners, reopened our trade routes, and commenced rebuilding our shattered cities.

DAWN

A raw, cold December morning in London. With the exception of a statuesque sentry on the Horse Guards' Parade, the wide open space was deserted. It had not long been light, and a heavy yellow mist still hung over the grass in St James's Park.

A bell clanged mournfully. Big Ben chimed the hour, and then boomed forth eight o'clock. An icy wind swept across the gravelled square. The, bare, black branches of the stunted trees creaked and groaned, and the lonely sentry standing at ease before his box rubbed his hands and shivered.

Suddenly a side door opened, and there emerged a small procession. Slowly there walked in front a clergyman bare-headed, reciting with solemn intonation the Burial Service. Behind him, with unsteady step and bent shoulders, a trembling man with blanched, haggard face, and a wild look of terror in his dark, deep-sunken eyes. He wore a shabby morning-coat tightly buttoned, and his hands in bracelets of steel were behind his back.

Glancing furtively around at the grey dismal landscape, he shuddered. Beside and behind him soldiers tramped on in silence.

The officer's sword grated along the gravel.

Suddenly a word of command caused them to halt against

a wall, and a sergeant, stepping forward, took a handkerchief and tied it over the eyes of the quivering culprit, who now stood with his back against the wall. Another word from the officer, and the party receded some distance, leaving the man alone. The monotonous nasal utterances of the chaplain still sounded as four privates advanced, and, halting, stood in single rank before the prisoner.

They raised their rifles. There was a momentary pause. In the distance a dog howled dismally.

A sharp word of command broke the quiet.

Then, a second later, as four rifles rang out simultaneously, the condemned man tottered forward and fell heavily on the gravel, shot through the heart.

It was the spy and murderer, Karl von Beilstein!

He had been brought from Glasgow to London in order that certain information might be elicited from him, and after his actions had been thoroughly investigated by a military court, he had been sentenced to death. The whole of his past was revealed by his valet Grevel, and it was proved that, in addition to bringing the great disaster upon England, he had also betrayed the country whose roubles purchased his cunningly-obtained secrets.

Geoffrey Engleheart, although gallantly assisting in the fight outside Leatherhead, and subsequently showing conspicuous bravery during the Battle of Caterham, fortunately escaped with nothing more severe than a bullet wound in the arm. During the searching private inquiry held at the Foreign Office after peace was restored, he explained the whole of the circumstances, and was severely reprimanded for his indiscretion; but as no suspicion of von Beilstein's real motive had been aroused prior to the Declaration of War, and as it was proved that Geoffrey was entirely innocent of any complicity in the affair, he was, at the urgent request of Lord Stanbury, allowed to resume his duties. Shortly afterwards he was married to Violet Vayne, and Sir Joseph, having recovered those of his ships that had been seized by the Russian Government, was thereby enabled to give his daughter a handsome dowry.

The young French clerk who had been engaged at the Admiralty, and who had committed murder for gold, escaped to Spain, and, after being hunted by English and Spanish detectives for many weeks, he became apparently overwhelmed by remorse. Not daring to show himself by day, nor to claim the money that had been promised him, he had tramped on through the snow from village to village in the unfrequented valleys of Lerida, while his description was being circulated throughout the Continent. Cold, weary, and hungry, he one night entered the Posada de las Pijorras at the little town of Oliana, at the foot of the Sierra del Cadi. Calling for wine, he took up a dirty crumpled copy of the Madrid *Globo*, three days old. A paragraph, headed 'The Missing Spy', caught his eyes, and, reading eagerly, he found to his dismay that the police were aware that he had been in Huesca a week before, and were now using bloodhounds to track him!

The paper fell from his nerveless grasp. The wine at his elbow he swallowed at one gulp, and, tossing down his last real upon the table, he rose and stumbled away blindly into the darkness.

When the wintry dawn spread in that silent, distant valley, it showed a corpse lying in the snow with face upturned. In the white wrinkled brow was a small dark-blue hole from which blood had oozed over the pallid cheek, leaving an ugly stain. The staring eyes were wide open, with a look of unutterable horror in them, and beside the thin clenched hand lay a revolver, one chamber of which had been discharged!

The dreary gloom of winter passed, and there dawned a new era of prosperity for England.

Dark days were succeeded by a period of happiness and rejoicing, and Britannia, grasping her trident again, seated herself on her shield beside the sea, Ruler of the Waves, Queen of Nations, and Empress of the World.